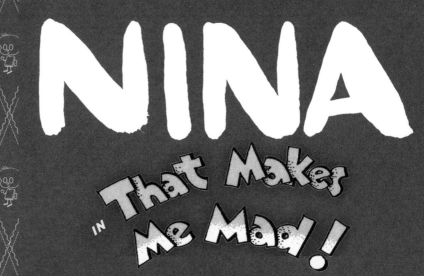

NINA

in That Makes Me Mad!

HILARY KNIGHT
STEVEN KROLL

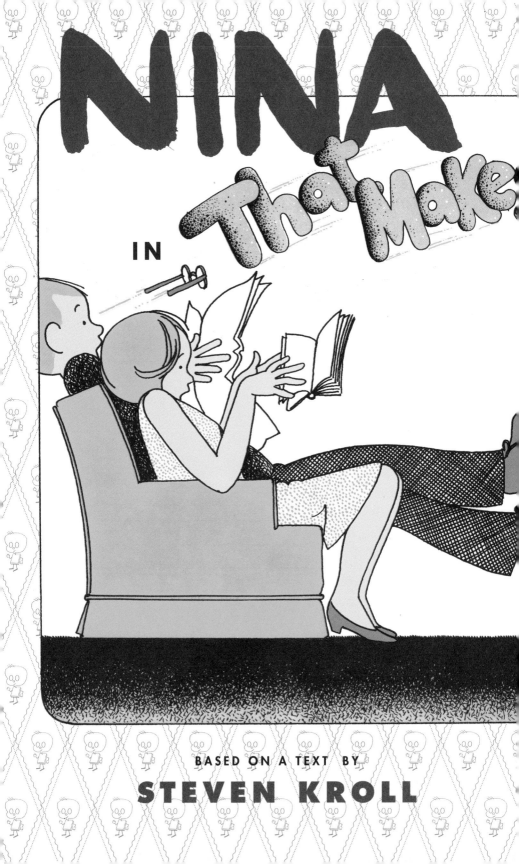

BASED ON A TEXT BY

STEVEN KROLL

A TOON BOOK BY

HILARY KNIGHT

TOON BOOKS IS AN IMPRINT OF CANDLEWICK PRESS

For my father, Clayton Knight
–Hilary Knight

For Kathleen. Forever.
–Steven Kroll

In memory of Steven Kroll (1941-2011),
a beloved and long-time member of
the children's book community.

Editorial Director: FRANÇOISE MOULY

Book Design: FRANÇOISE MOULY & LAURA FOXGROVER

A TOON Book™ © 2011 RAW Junior, LLC, 27 Greene Street, New York, NY 10013. TOON Books® is an imprint of Candlewick Press, 99 Dover Street, Somerville, MA 02144. Original text © 1976 Steven Kroll. Original illustrations © 1976 by Hilary Knight. No part of this book may be used or reproduced in any manner whatsoever without written permission except in the case of brief quotations embodied in critical articles and reviews. TOON Books®, LITTLE LIT® and TOON Into Reading™ are trademarks of RAW Junior, LLC. All rights reserved. Printed in Singapore by Tien Wah Press (Pte.) Ltd.

Library of Congress Cataloging-in-Publication Data:
Knight, Hilary.
  Nina in That makes me mad : a TOON book / by Hilary Knight ; based on a text by Steven Kroll.
    p. cm.
Summary: Lots of little, everyday frustrations make Nina mad, and she is very good at expressing her feelings.
ISBN-13: 978-1-935179-10-8 (hardcover) ISBN-10: 1-935179-10-1 (hardcover)
  1. Graphic novels. [1. Graphic novels. 2. Anger–Fiction. 3. Behavior–Fiction.] I. Kroll, Steven. II. Title. III. Title: That makes me mad.
PZ7.7.K66Ni 2011
741.5'973–dc22
                            2011000802
              ISBN 13: 978-1-935179-10-8 ISBN 10: 1-935179-10-1

         12 13 14 15 16 17 TWP 10 9 8 7 6 5 4 3

11

When I do something nice and no one cares...

...that makes me **MAD**!

ABOUT THE AUTHORS

HILARY KNIGHT is the son of two accomplished artist-writers, Clayton Knight and Katherine Sturges, who collaborated on this classic *New Yorker* cover (Katherine penciled and Clayton inked it.) Hilary Knight came into his own enormous success by illustrating Kay Thompson's *Eloise*, which has been a cultural touchstone for generations. He has written and illustrated nine children's books and illustrated over fifty more. He has also produced many magazine illustrations, record-album covers, and posters for Broadway musicals.

STEVEN KROLL wrote nearly a hundred books for children. He has said, "When I'm working on a book, I see the pictures as I write the words. How fortunate that the illustrators of my books have all seen what I've seen and have captured the magic I wish to share."

TIPS FOR PARENTS AND TEACHERS:

HOW TO READ COMICS WITH KIDS

Kids *love* comics! They are naturally drawn to the details in the pictures, which make them want to read the words. Comics beg for repeated readings and let both emerging and reluctant readers enjoy complex stories with a rich vocabulary. But since comics have their own grammar, here are a few tips for reading them with kids:

GUIDE YOUNG READERS: Use your finger to show your place in the text, but keep it at the bottom of the speaking character so it doesn't hide the very important facial expressions.

HAM IT UP! Think of the comic book story as a play and don't hesitate to read with expression and intonation. Assign parts or get kids to supply the sound effects, a great way to reinforce phonics skills.

LET THEM GUESS. Comics provide a lot of context for the words, so the emerging readers can make informed guesses. Like jigsaw puzzles, comics ask readers to make connections, so check a young audience's understanding by asking "What's this character thinking?" (but don't be surprised if a kid finds some of the comics' subtle details faster than you).

TALK ABOUT THE PICTURES. Point out how the artist paces the story with pauses (silent panels) or speeded-up action (a burst of short panels). Discuss how the size and shape of the panels carry meaning.

ABOVE ALL, ENJOY! There is of course never one right way to read, so go for the shared pleasure. Once children make the story happen in their imagination, they have discovered the thrill of reading, and you won't be able to stop them. At that point, just go get them more books, and more comics.

www.TOON-BOOKS.com

SEE OUR FREE ONLINE CARTOON MAKERS,
LESSON PLANS, AND MUCH MORE

3 1901 03694 7762